LITTLE RED
AND THE
BIG, BAD,
SEXY WOLF

LACY JANE

LACY JANE

Little Red and the Big, Bad, Sexy Wolf

(Once Upon a Time: Twisted Sexy Fairy Tales—Book 2)

Contents

One

Scarlett

Once upon a time, there was a girl named Scarlett. She was on her way to her grandma's house, not knowing that she was about to meet a big, bad, sexy wolf.

I am driving up the steep mountain road to meet Granny's realtor at her house. Granny took a vacation to Miami last month and loved it so much, she decided to move there. She came home, packed everything up, and was on her way. Which brings me to now. She asked me to show her house to Mr. Wolf, the realtor she randomly chose. After everything Granny has done for me, it's really the least that I can do. Considering she raised me as her own after my folks took off for parts unknown right after I was born, I kind of owe her. She is pretty much the only parent I have had for all of my twenty-two years. Granny is my favorite person in the world. I miss her already. I don't mind helping her out; really, I don't. My Mini Cooper just wasn't made for these steep mountain roads.

When I finally make it to Granny's cabin, I see that someone is already there, waiting on the front porch. I get out of my car, but when the man turns around to face me, I freeze. He is a behemoth of a man; well over six feet tall. He has sun kissed skin with short black hair, and a sexy beard I'd love to run my fingers through . He is wearing a suit that surely had to be custom made to fit his massive shoulders and chest. His eyes are a really odd amber color. They almost look like they are glowing.

The man is drop dead gorgeous, but it's not just that. I have never had any kind of attraction to anyone before, but this man is doing it for me in spades. I take a few steps toward him, and he makes an odd noise. Did he just growl at me?

Moisture pools between my legs. Damn. That has seriously never happened to me before. He takes a whiff of the air and suddenly looks ravenous. There is no way that he can know I'm wet. Right? I try to discreetly rub my legs together to get some relief, but it doesn't seem to help the ache any. I attempt to regain my composure, and approach him with an outstretched hand. "Hi. I'm Scarlett Jones; Daisy's granddaughter," I manage to squeak out.

He licks his lips. "I'm Damian Wolf," he says in his very husky voice. "Everyone just calls me Wolf, but you should call me Damian," he says, running his fingers down my neck, giving me goosebumps all over, and making my panties spontaneously combust. "I guess that makes you little red, and me, the big, bad wolf." He stares at me for so long, I feel like I'm in a trance. Instead of shaking my hand, he lifts it to his lips for a kiss. Shock waves roll through me and set every nerve in my body on fire. He spreads kisses across the top of my hand, shooting desire through my system and making me breathless. He tugs me closer, putting his mouth against my ear, and making it seem very warm outside despite the dropping temperature. "You might not realize it yet, but sweetheart? You. Are. Mine."

I don't think I can say no to this man. I don't even want to. I am so fucked.

Two

Damian

Scarlett takes a deep breath and giggles nervously. She might think I'm kidding, but I'm not. I've been on this earth for forty-five years waiting for my fated mate. The second I looked at her, I was a goner. I couldn't have picked a more perfect match if I tried. She has pouty pink lips that I imagine wrapped around my cock, emerald green eyes that shine with merriment, and a cute dusting of freckles across her face. She has shiny ginger curls flowing to her waist, pale skin, and a curvy body just made to be fucked and bred. She will be able to handle the constant pounding I plan on giving her. She looks sweet and innocent, and I can't wait to dirty her up.

In case you don't know, wolves mate for life-not only normal wolves, but also wolf shifters, like myself. When a shifter finds his mate, her scent is intoxicating to him; the most delicious smell imaginable. I scoffed at that description before, thinking it was an exaggeration, but now I'm a believer. The second I caught a whiff of my gorgeous mate, I nearly stopped breathing. Now that I can smell her arousal, it is taking everything in me not to just throw her down and claim her. I'm having a really tough time holding back like I need to. I know that humans generally need more time than us to get used to the whole mate concept. I'm trying to give her a few minutes to catch up. I can't seem to keep my hands off of her, though. I breathe in her delicious scent, running my hand down the back of her neck.

Scarlett pulls away and shakily unlocks the front door, giving the first hint that I've rattled her. She has no idea at the restraint it is taking for me to not just throw her down on the floor and give her the hard fucking she deserves. She closes the door behind us and starts rattling off information about the cabin. I have a feeling that she talks nonstop when she is nervous.

I really don't give a shit about the listing anymore. From now on, all I care about is her-my perfect mate. My cock is standing at attention for the first time in my life. A wolf shifter can only be aroused by his or her mate, and let me tell you, my little red is arousing the hell out of me right now without even trying.

She nervously licks her lips, and my control is shot. I stalk toward her, hearing her shallow breaths. She is aroused by me, but nervous. She doesn't understand that she belongs to me now. The pull we feel toward each other is probably overwhelming for her.

I put my hand on the back of her neck, pulling her toward me. I kiss her lips gently, then her neck; licking the spot I will be biting very soon. Her pulse accelerates as she shifts her legs and pulls me closer. I can feel her nipples pebble against her bra. "Fuck, yes! You are mine. I need you, Scarlett. Now," I say, thrusting my hard cock against her.

Three

Scarlett

What is happening to me? I was a normal girl up until a few minutes ago. Now I'm so turned on, I can't think straight. Since I set eyes on Damian, I can't think of anything but him. His touch sets me on fire.

"Has anyone else ever touched you like this, sweetheart?" he asks while stroking his hands up and down my body. I shake my head. I've never had any interest in anyone before. I'd never even been kissed until a few seconds ago. I don't understand why this man is making me feel so out of control. Sure, he's gorgeous, but it's more than that. I don't understand why I'm letting a man I just met seduce me. He grazes his fingertip over my engorged nipple before pinching it hard, causing me to orgasm.

"Oh, god! What am I doing?" I push him away from me, trying to regain my composure. Damn, he's hot. He could get any woman he wanted, and probably does. This is probably a common occurrence for him. I bet he uses his seductive powers on unsuspecting women every day. The thought pisses me off way more than it should.

"This is not a one time thing, sweetheart. We are made for each other. You are my fated mate. You are the only woman for me, and I am the only man for you. You are the woman I will spend my life with. The one I will kiss, touch, fuck every day, make babies with, and grow old with."

My heart is beating out of my chest. There's no way he's for real, right? People don't just set eyes on someone and know that it's their "one". Do they?

"Come here, Scarlett." He crooks his finger at me. He's like a force field, pulling me in. I feel hypnotized, unable to disobey his command, as I walk back to him.

"Good girl," he breathes against my ear, sending shivers down my spine and ruining my panties. He kisses my ear and neck gently, slowly making his way back around to my lips. His mouth barely touches mine, but electricity shoots through my entire body, awakening desires that I didn't even know I possessed. After a few seconds, the kiss becomes more urgent. His tongue tangles with mine. He picks me up like I weigh nothing, and holds me up against the wall while he takes my mouth over and over. He starts grinding his enormous hard cock against my pussy, causing me to explode again.

"Fuck, baby. You feel so good. I can't wait to be inside you." He pulls up my skirt, and rips my panties off. Damn. That is so hot! I should be outraged, but I am even more turned on than before. He slips his fingers inside my pussy lips, stroking me. I love feeling his hands and mouth on me. He pushes his fingers in harder, causing me to cry out again. He pulls them out and and licks my juices off of them like they are a delicacy. I am completely lost in the sensations he is sending through my body. "So responsive. So wet for me."

I'm ready to surrender until I look up and see his eyes glowing; like, literally glowing. It snaps me out of the spell I've been under. "What the fuck, Damian?" I push him away again. "What is wrong with your eyes?"

"My wolf is trying to break through and get to you. He's happy that we've found our mate."

Damn. He would have to be delusional. "Riiight. Your wolf. Okey dokey."

"You don't believe me."

"It doesn't matter what I believe."

"I only care about what you believe, sweetheart. Here, let me show you," he says, quickly shucking his clothes, and causing me to nearly hyperventilate.

"What are you doing?" I ask breathlessly, trying not to stare at his giant, muscular physique.

"I'm introducing you to my wolf."

Suddenly, his whole body contorts, and his bones make terrible popping noises. "Oh my god! What the hell?" Okay. So, apparently he isn't delusional after all. I am frozen in place as I take in the giant gray wolf now standing casually in Granny's cabin. I pinch myself to see if I'm dreaming. Nope. Not dreaming. I should be terrified, but I'm somehow soothed by the furry creature. He comes toward me, nudging me with his nose. I stroke his fur, causing him to purr noisily. I feel confident that he would never harm me.

"Is this seriously you?" He comes closer and licks my face, causing me to giggle again. If you would have told me a day ago that a wolf would lick my face and I would laugh about it, I would have thought you were stoned.

It only takes a few seconds for the wolf to morph back into the sexy man I met earlier. Only now, I can't help but notice his lack of clothing. It makes it really hard for me to pay attention to anything else. My eyes are fixated on the hard beast between his legs. I felt his cock against me earlier, but seeing it in all its glory? Whoa. It's enormous; so thick and long. It looks purple and angry, and is dripping cream from the tip. The ache between my legs intensifies. I am suddenly dying for a taste of Damian's giant cock. I try to look anywhere else, but I just can't help myself. I have never been so turned on.

He smiles at me like he can read what's going on in my dirty little mind. "You are welcome to explore me all you want, sweetheart, but I'm not sure you are ready for that yet. Would you feel more comfortable if I were dressed?"

"Definitely."

He quickly puts his clothes back on. "What do you know about shifters, baby?"

I know that this one is hot as fuck, but I don't say that. "Nothing, apparently. Up until a few minutes ago, I thought they were fictional."

"No. We are very real. There are a lot of us here, though we try to stay under the radar. When we find our fated mate, we mate for life. The first time I take you, I will mark you with my bite. That will complete our mating ritual, and let other shifters know that you are taken. There is only one fated mate for each shifter, and you are mine," he states as he kisses the side of my neck, making his way toward my aching breasts. I so badly want to just give in to my desire, giving us both what we want, but I need some space to clear my head first. That is the logical thing to do. Right?

I force myself to pull away. "I need some time," I say quietly. I see the disappointment on his face. I move further away, and feel like I'm missing a huge part of myself. Maybe this pull will go away when I'm not looking at his gorgeous face and body.

"I'm not happy about it, but I do understand. It's a lot for you to digest. Let me see your phone." I hand it over to him. "I'm programming my number in. I'll give you some time to come to terms with this. Call me when you are ready, or if you need anything. I will answer any questions you have. You can call me anytime, day or night, and I will be there."

"Okay," I say. I kiss him on the cheek, then flee like the hounds of hell are after me.

Four

Scarlett

"My house. ASAP. Bring ice cream. 911," I text my bestie, Goldie. She is the only one I can think of to talk to about this. We met a few years ago when she moved to town to be with her husbands. Yes, husbands, plural. She has three. It sounds a little crazy, but the three giant brothers are obsessed with her and vice versa. There have been several times that I saw way more than I should have since her men can't seem to keep their hands off of her.

I met Goldie at the library's romance book club, and we bonded over our love of steamy romance novels and coffee drinks. She is with her men most of the time, but we still hang out a lot and talk on the phone nearly every day. She also has two-year-old triplets that I love to spoil. I'm their honorary auntie.

"On my way!" she texts back.

Ten minutes after I walk inside my house, Goldie is at the door. She gives me a tight hug. "Okay. Spill. What is going on that calls for ice cream?" She sets a few containers on the counter, and I grab two spoons.

"Have you ever heard of shifters?" I ask, taking a bite of my Haagen Daaz chocolate ice cream. So delicious!

Goldie suddenly looks uncomfortable. "Yes. Why do you ask?"

"Because I just met Granny's realtor, Damian Wolf, and he's a wolf shifter who says he's my fated mate and we are going to be together forever," I get out in one long breath.

"You are his mate? Oh my god! That is so great! I'm so happy for you!" She jumps up and down, then gives me another hug before pulling away. "Wait a sec. If you found each other, why are you here with me and not off with him?"

"I didn't even know shifters were real until about thirty minutes ago. I told him I needed a little space."

"Oh, honey. He's going to be busting down your door any second now. We'd better talk fast," she says while licking her spoonful of rocky road.

"So, you know about shifters?"

"Yep. That's fair to say."

"Do you know any?" I can tell by her silence that she does. "Who?"

"Well, we live in a town with a pretty big shifter population. There are tons of them. But the ones I know best are my husbands."

"What?!" I screech. "Oh my god! I can't believe you never told me!"

"I'm so sorry! They are really weird about it. The only people I've told are my parents, and now you."

"Are they wolves, too?"

"No. They are grizzly bears."

"Wow. Did it not freak you out to have that sprung on you?"

"Not at all. I had dreams about them for years before I found them, so I knew what I was getting into."

"So, when you are their fated mate, what's it like?"

"It is wonderful! They are obsessed with you. They don't want anyone else. They will do everything in their power to make you happy. And the sex? Oh. My. God. You will never want to get out of bed. They are also possessive as hell."

I have noticed that her husbands are crazy protective of her. They do seem to growl a lot, too. It all makes a lot of sense now that I think about it. "So you think that this is okay? I'm not crazy for jumping into a relationship with a man I just met?"

"Oh, honey. It would be crazy not to be with him if he's your mate. I'm telling you, it's the best thing in the world. It puts the romance novels we read to shame."

She puts the ice cream in my freezer for next time. "Now go get your wolf!" she says as she walks out the door.

"I will. Thank you." I give Goldie another hug, then go inside to freshen up. I send Damian a text to meet me here. I check my hair and makeup. My entire body hums with anticipation.

Five

Damian

I told Scarlett I would give her time, but my beast is already trying to break through and mark her. I won't be able to hold him back much longer. I got her address and am standing outside her cottage, pacing back and forth.

Goldie, the Bear brothers' wife, leaves and heads toward her car. They must be good friends if Scarlett invited her over. That bodes well since she is mated to three bear shifters. Maybe she can make Scarlett understand just how special finding your mate is. She turns and grins at me. "Bye, Wolf! Congratulations!" I smile and wave back at her.

I am doing everything I can to hold myself back when a text from Scarlett comes through on my phone, asking me to come over. I am ringing her doorbell seconds later.

"Damian! How on earth did you get here so fast?"

"I was already here. Waiting."

She smiles, sealing her fate. I push her inside with my body, slam the door, then push her up against it. "Have you learned a little more about shifters and mates, babe?" I ask, kissing her gently.

"Yes. I know a little more now," she says, closing her eyes. "I don't really understand all of this, but I don't want to stay away from you any longer. I ache for you."

"You have no idea how happy that makes me, sweetheart." She just gave me permission, and my beast is through waiting. I tear her dress open, making buttons fly in every direction. I rip her bra off, baring her succulent breasts. I squeeze her luscious tits, taking turns sucking on her sweet strawberry nipples until she climaxes.

"Damian!" She screams.

I caress every inch of her curvy body. Her skin feels like silk, and smells like vanilla and cinnamon. I take her mouth again, licking inside, and pulling her closer. "Where's your bedroom, sweetheart?"

"First door on the left." I pick her up and rush to her bedroom. I toss her on the bed, and rip her dress the rest of the way off, baring her gorgeous curves. Her perfect little pussy is bare and glistening with her juices.

"Mine," I growl, before devouring her sweetness with my mouth. Scarlett's scent is intoxicating, but her taste is even better. I will happily lick this sweet little cunt for the rest of my life. She screams again, gushing against my face. I tear off my shirt, then undo my slacks as quickly as possible. My big cock is already dripping pre-cum, ready to go.

She is lying on the bed, legs spread wide open, just waiting for me. Her large tits and tiny waist draw my attention. She has the perfect body. Perfect for fucking, and perfect for carrying and nursing my babies.

"So, I guess everything happens really fast with shifters and their mates?" she asks breathlessly, writhing on the bed.

"Yes, sweetheart. It does. You are my mate. I'm going to spend the next several days showing you that we are made for each other. I'm going to fuck you so good, you'll never want to get out of bed." She gushes again. Damn. She likes dirty talk. I am one lucky shifter.

Her eyes rake over me in appreciation. I can smell her arousal. It's driving me insane. I spend a little time loosening her up with my fingers and tongue. There's a lot of me to take, and I don't want to hurt my beautiful mate.

"Damn, baby. You are sopping wet for me." When I can't wait a second longer, I push the tip of my cock into her wet opening and enter heaven.

Six

Scarlett

Oh my god. I've never been so turned on. Damian is so sexy. I feel like I will die if I don't have him all the way inside me right this second. His giant cock is stretching me. I know pain is coming, but I don't care. I've never wanted anything so badly in all my life.

"Yes, Damian! More! Fuck me!"

"Fuck, Scarlett. You feel so good. Your sweet little pussy is squeezing the life out my cock, but you will take every inch of me. Once you do, I may never leave your hot little cunt."

With that, he pushes all the way in. It stings for a few seconds, but then I feel more pleasure than I could have ever imagined.

"I'm sorry, baby. I don't want to hurt you."

"I'm good now. Please don't stop."

"Never," he says. His eyes glow as he pounds into me harder and harder, making me lightheaded from orgasm after orgasm. "Mine!" he yells as he takes me, slamming the bed against the wall over and over again with the force of his thrusts. My neck starts tingling like crazy. He licks the exact place that tingles before biting me there. I feel pain for a moment, then even more pleasure as he explodes inside me, triggering one last orgasm from me, and sending me into a deep sleep.

A short time later, I feel Damian cleaning me with a damp washcloth. He is so sweet. I want to tell him that, but I can't keep my eyes open.

Seven

Scarlett

I wake up feeling very confused. Why am in bed in the middle of the day? I roll over and land against Damian. Oh, right. That really wasn't a dream. I actually did have sex with a man I just met a few hours ago. A man who is apparently my fated mate.

I know this would sound crazy to anyone else, but as I take in Wolf's incredible body, I have no regrets. I know that I would absolutely, one hundred percent, do it all over again. He rolls onto his back, dislodging the covers. His beast of a cock is standing at attention, causing my mouth to water and moisture to pool between my legs.

I don't understand what is happening to me. Up until a short while ago, I had never had any interest whatsoever in having sex with anyone. I kind of thought I was asexual, but apparently not. I just had to find my mate to become a full fledged sex fiend. I am already starving for him again. Before I even realize what I'm doing, I move down his body and suck the tip of his cock into my mouth, making him moan. I am so hungry for him, I can't help myself.

"You taste so good," I say, swirling my tongue around his cock head like a lollipop.

"Damn, Scarlett. That feels so good, baby. Keep sucking that big cock," he says, pushing my mouth farther down on him. He soon loses control and starts fucking my mouth hard. I am having a tough time keeping up, but I love it. My eyes water, and my throat burns, but I love that Damian is so out of control. "Gonna come down your throat now." His dick hits the back of my throat and explodes. I greedily swallow every creamy drop. I barely touch my clit and come right along with him.

"Fuck, baby. That's a hell of a way to wake a man up," he says, trying to catch his breath.

"I don't seem to have any self control around you," I say, tracing patterns across his hairy chest.

"Believe me; the feeling is mutual."

Before I know it, I'm flat on my back again being fucked hard by my delicious man. He slams inside me repeatedly, causing the bed to creak hard, until it finally breaks.

"Oh, my god! I can't believe we broke the bed!" I giggle. It only takes me a second to forget all about it. Wolf throws the mattress on the floor like it weighs nothing, before tossing me on top of it and fucking me so hard I see stars.

Eight

Damian

When I open my eyes, it's morning. I see my beautiful mate lying next to me. I stroke her cheek, then run my hands over her hips. Her porcelain skin shows scrapes and bruises from being taken so hard. That should bother me, but being the beast I am, I love seeing my marks on her. I know that she'll be feeling me whenever she walks; not only today, but always. I will never let her forget who she belongs to.

"Is it morning?" she asks, smiling up at me.

"It is, angel. I'd fix you some breakfast, but I'm a terrible cook."

"Good thing I'm a great cook," she says, jumping out of bed.

A short while later, my little red has laid out quite a spread for us-omelettes, pancakes, toast, and fruit. "This looks so good, sweetheart. Thank you. I'd say it is too much, but we both probably need some sustenance after yesterday."

She blushes adorably. "You are probably right. I am starving!"

We sit next to each other at her kitchen table. She tells me all about her job at the library, while I tell her about being a realtor. The conversation flows smoothly, never feeling forced or uncomfortable. We learn a lot about each other in a short time.

She's only wearing my shirt. She looks way better in it than I have ever thought about looking. When she finishes eating, she starts putting things in the dishwasher. When she bends over, I see that she has no panties on. I am on her in a flash.

"Oh! Damian!" she gasps as I bend her over and devour her sweet little cunt with my mouth. I put her on the kitchen island and lick her honey hole. It doesn't take long before she is begging for me.

"Please fuck me, Damian." I free my hungry cock and push inside, causing her to gasp.

"Are you too sore, baby?"

"No! Please don't stop."

"Not a chance," I say as I slam into her velvet heat faster and faster. It doesn't take long for her to come again. When her pussy pulses hard and squeezes my cock, it's all I can take. I let go, spilling stream after stream of cum inside my mate, and hoping that she is already pregnant.

Nine

Scarlett

Later that day, we stop by Damian's to pick up some clothes for him. I look around as we walk inside. It's a nice place, but a little cold. No pictures, no paintings. The walls are completely bare.

"Sorry. I just moved in a short time ago, and haven't done any decorating. I didn't know I'd be bringing my mate home with me," he says nervously.

"It's fine," I reassure him with a quick kiss. Well, it was supposed to be a quick kiss. Before I know it, I have my clothes peeled off of me and am being flipped over on my hands and knees on his couch.

"It's been too long, sweetheart," he says as he massages my ass before slamming his cock in me from behind. "Yes!" we both cry out. "I'll never get enough of this sweet little pussy." Oh, god. His dirty talk really does it for me; just like everything else about him. "You are drenched, baby. You want my big cock fucking you?"

"Yes!" I scream. He slams into me again and again. My climax hits me suddenly. My pussy tightens around him hard, making him pour inside me. He pulls out, then picks me up like I weigh nothing.

"Little red, I think I need to give you a tour of my bedroom."

"Lead on, my big, bad, sexy wolf."

Ten

Damian

Some time later, we are lying in bed resting.

"Whose house?" I ask, thinking out loud.

"Whose house for what?"

"Whose house should we live in; mine or yours?"

"Whoa. We literally just met each other yesterday! Don't you think this is way too fast?"

"Baby, this is it. This is the real deal. You are it for me, and I am it for you. I have no doubts. There's no reason to wait. I want to move in together, wife you up, and put my baby in you as soon as possible."

"Oh, shit!" she says as it suddenly dawns on her. "We haven't used any protection!"

"No, we haven't. I will be thrilled if you are pregnant. I have been doing everything I can to knock you up."

She laughs. "You definitely have been filling me up every chance you get. I would love to have a baby with you, too. How about if we just live at my place for now and maybe build sometime down the road?"

"Works for me, sweetheart. Now, how soon can I get you to the altar?"

Eleven

Scarlett

The answer is soon; very soon. I am getting ready for my wedding one week after meeting Damian Wolf. One week! It sounds insane, but it feels right. When you know, you know. If you are not with a shifter, it's just a little tough to understand. And if you are, lucky you!

Goldie and Granny zip up my dress. As I look at my reflection in the mirror, I've never felt so beautiful. I look like a princess with my gorgeous white gown that glitters with my every move. I glow with happiness, and it's all because of my handsome fiance.

A short while later, I am walking down the aisle to a very sexy, and very impatient, Damian. "It's about time. I was about to come find you," he says, kissing my cheek. "You look stunning."

"Thank you, baby. You look very handsome." All dressed in a tux, he looks scrumptious. His biceps are testing the strength of his sleeves. He looks like he might hulk out and bust through at any time. As he takes my hand, I realize I have no doubts whatsoever that this is who I want to spend my life with. It doesn't matter how quickly it happened. I know that he is my person.

After a speedy ceremony, the minister pronounces us husband and wife, and Damian lays a borderline x-rated kiss on me. He holds the back of my neck while his mouth takes mine over and over again until I can't think straight. We are wrapped in each others arms, oblivious to everything else. Finally, the minister clearing his throat breaks through my haze of lust. My face gets a little red, but I don't care too much. I wouldn't change anything about my sexy husband, including his very public claiming of me.

"To be continued," he whispers in my ear.

"I can't wait."

Twelve

Damian

For a small reception, there are a lot of people here. Apparently, most of our small town came out for the wedding. It's great that people are so friendly here; don't get me wrong. The problem is I need inside my wife. Now. She insisted that we spend the night before our wedding apart. I was not too happy about it. It's the first night I've slept alone since finding her, and it will be the last one if I have anything to say about it.

Scarlett is across the room talking to some people I don't recognize. I stalk over to her and take her hand. "Baby, can you help me with something really quick?"

"Sure," she smiles up at me.

I'm practically dragging her to a small room in the back of the chapel. "Where are we going?"

I shut us in, and push her against the door. "I need your sweet pussy right now." I push up the poofy dress to get to her.

"Yesss," she hisses as I push her panties to the side and sink my fingers inside her wetness. "Damian!" she screams, gushing on my fingers. I lick them clean.

"So fucking delicious." She licks her lips as I undo my pants. My cock springs out, slapping against my stomach. I'm already dripping pre-cum. I can't get inside my bride quick enough. "Come lie down on the couch. Hold your dress up and spread your legs. Let us have a quick preview of our honeymoon."

She does what I tell her. Within seconds, I am pumping in and out of her sweet pussy. I know that neither of us are going to last long. When she screams again, her sweet little cunt milks every drop of cum out of me. We lie there for a few minutes, catching our breath.

"Come on, sweetheart," I say, pulling her up. We straighten her dress out the best we can, and try not to look like we just ducked out of our reception to have sex. Considering how many shifters are here, they probably already know. I give her another kiss to tide us over. "Let's get this reception over with so we can start our honeymoon."

Thirteen

Scarlett

The reception went on longer than either of us would have liked, but it was pretty awesome to have all of our friends and family in one place. We are finally back at my house. We are leaving for our honeymoon in Bora Bora tomorrow.

"Come here, little red," Damian says in his sexy voice.

"Me? What could the big, bad, sexy wolf possibly want with little old me?" I say, helping my new husband out of his dress clothes.

"Everything."

"Oh, my, Mr. Wolf. What big, strong arms you have."

"The better to hold you with, my dear."

"What big hands you have."

"The better to touch you with, my dear."

"What big teeth you have."

"The better to eat you with, my dear." He grins, stripping his underwear off. His cock is at full attention; dripping and ready for me.

"Oh, Mr. Wolf, what a big, hard cock you have!" I say, stroking him, and licking his pre-cum from my fingers.

"The better to fuck you with, my dear," he says, tossing me down on the bed. I giggle, then help him take my dress off before he destroys it like he has way too many of my clothes already.

"There's a zipper on the side."

"Good thing. This dress was about to be ripped off your sexy little body." He unzips my dress and sets it on an armchair before returning to me. "Now, little red, you are all mine. You look sexy as fuck in this outfit."

I smile as he kisses and teases his way down my sexy bridal lingerie, complete with garters and stockings. He kisses my mouth before working his way down my neck and chest, eliciting appreciative moans from me. He drags my teddy down, cupping my breasts and sucking them. I arch off the bed with the pleasure of it. He tosses the garment over his shoulder. I move to take off my thigh high stockings.

"Leave them on while I fuck you. They are sexy as hell, baby."

"As you wish." His mouth zeroes in on my pussy, devouring me whole. "Oh, my god!" His tongue laps at me, drinking down my orgasms and setting me off again. He bites down on my clit and I come hard, screaming his name.

While I'm catching my breath, he climbs on top of me. "I'm nowhere near done with you, sweetheart," he says as he thrusts his throbbing cock inside me, causing me to gush again. "I'll never get enough of you, Scarlett. You are mine. Now and always."

"And you are mine," I say, coming again. "Fuck me harder, baby."

"Your wish is my command," he says, thrusting even harder. I feel his body tense before he gushes inside of me, sending me into another orgasm.

"I love you so much, Mrs. Wolf."

"I love you, too, Mr. Wolf."

Fourteen

Epilogue–Scarlett

One year later...

What a difference a year makes. I have gone from being single and alone to being happily married with a gorgeous husband and our beautiful baby girl, Piper. Damian managed to get me pregnant right off the bat. She's an absolute angel, and looks like my mini me.

"Where are my beautiful girls?" My husband calls out, as he walks in the front door.

"Right here!" I call from the living room. He comes in and kisses Piper, then me.

"I've missed you, sweetheart."

I laugh. "It's only been two hours since you left."

"I know, but even that is too long."

"I missed you, too."

"Are you two up to going for a ride? There's something I want to show you."

A few minutes later, we load up in our roomy SUV, headed to a surprise destination. We soon pull up in front of a gorgeous home. "Where are we?"

"I want you to keep an open mind. I just got the listing for this house. I know we talked about building, but I think you will love this place."

He unhooks Piper's baby seat, swinging it slowly around, trying to keep her asleep for the time being. When we walk inside, I am stunned. If you had asked me to describe my dream house, this would be it. Soaring ceilings, a massive fireplace, wood beams, and a kitchen that Gordon Ramsey would be jealous of. "Wow! It's gorgeous!"

There is a huge backyard, and even a game room. He takes me through the rest of the house. There are five bedrooms, which we apparently need since Wolf is determined to keep me knocked up. I just had Piper a few months ago, but I'm already pregnant again, thanks to my ravenous husband and his super sperm.

"Well, what do you think?"

"I love it!"

"I'm so glad. I could picture us here as soon as I saw it. I'll put in an offer today. But first, I think we need to christen our new house."

"Ooh, I like the way you think."

Fifteen

Epilogue 2-Damian

Ten years later...

It's quiet in the house when I walk in, which is very unusual. With six kids, quiet just doesn't happen very often; or ever. A movement outside catches my eye. I walk out the back door and am greeted with chaos. This is more like it. Laughing, screaming, running. And wolves. Lots of wolves.

"There you are! Please deal with this. Your children are out of control." Scarlett says, while kissing me softly. When they are angels, they are hers. When they are a mess, they are mine. Our two youngest just started shifting last week. Now that all six of them can shift, they race around every chance they get, destroying everything in their path. Our patio furniture is strewn about and shredded. It looks like our backyard got hit by a tornado.

"Give me an hour, baby. I'll wear them out." I strip and change into my wolf form. I spend the next hour racing with the kids in the woods behind our house until they are finally beat. "Go take baths and get ready for bed." The kids all go inside, wrapping themselves in beach towels. A short while later, everyone is down for the count.

"Now it's time for this wolf to play with little red," I say as I close our bedroom door. Scarlett is under the covers, smiling mischievously at me.

"What could you possible want with me, Mr. Wolf?" she bats her eyelashes at me. She tosses the covers aside, revealing her gorgeous, naked body.

"Everything. I want everything with you," I growl, tossing my clothes aside and pinning my wife down in one quick move.

"You can have whatever you want from me," she says, thrusting her hips against my hardness. I'm already leaking pre-cum. Even after all these years, my wife turns me on without even trying. Within seconds, I'm inside her; my favorite place to be. I'm so lucky to have found my mate.

"Fuck, Scarlett. You feel too good. I'll never last."

"Then don't. Come inside me. Give me another baby."

That's all it takes. She knows that nothing makes me lose control like the idea of knocking her up. I pound into her until I feel her pussy pulsing and clenching hard around my cock. I let go, filling her with enough cum to make her pregnant twenty times over.

I curl her up against me. "I love you so much, Scarlett."

"I love you, too, Damian. I'm so glad I found my big, bad, sexy wolf."

He laughs. "And I'm so glad I found my beautiful, perfect, little red."

Little red and her wolf lived happily ever after.

The End

If you enjoyed this book, please take a few moments to write a review of it. Thank you!

37

More Twisted Sexy Fairy Tales are coming soon!

Sixteen

Preview–Goldie Locks and the Three Sexy Bear Shifters

Goldie

Once upon a time, there was a girl named Goldie Locks, who had very naughty dreams...

I'm not like other girls my age. While they daydream about the captain of the football team or the cute boy in their math class, I daydream about three bear shifters. Actually, I daydream, nightdream, all the time dream, and am fucking obsessed with them.

The first time I dreamt of them, I had just turned thirteen...

There were three huge bears standing at the foot of a massive bed. They stared at me so strangely, almost like they were starving for me. It should have frightened me, but instead it made my tummy flutter.

I woke up longing to see the bears again. I have had tons of dreams about playing outside with them, laughing and feeling so happy. I have dreamt about them regularly over the years, but the dreams have happened more frequently and become much, much dirtier over the last few months.

I should introduce myself. I'm Goldie Locks. Seriously. My parents both have a really twisted sense of humor and thought it would be hilarious to name me Goldie. Now the joke is on them since I'm obsessed with three bears. Ha ha.

Since I turned eighteen last month, the dreams have become a nightly thing. They have gotten to the point that they take over the second I fall asleep. One of the dreams I have the most often, I had again last night…

I'm lying on a massive bed. The three men rush into the room in their bear forms. They stare at me as if they want to feast on me, but I know that they are not dangerous to me. They swiftly morph into the sexy men I've been dreaming about for years. Three men, so similar, yet so different.

They are all huge; at least six foot eight or nine. They have muscles upon muscles and are much broader than other men. Their hair is jet black, and their eyes are nearly black, too, with flecks of gold. They have neatly trimmed beards that I know will tickle when they kiss me. Their arms are massive, like they live in the gym, and their chests are ripped, too, with just enough hair to be sexy to the extreme. They each have that awesome vee that some men have that points down to their huge cocks. Wow. And yum. They are obviously brothers, but I can easily tell them apart despite the fact that they look so similar with their tan skin and dark hair.

I look down at their monstrous, hard cocks and feel moisture pool between my legs. They want me just as desperately as I want them. "Please," I beg them, writhing on the bed. They waste no time in ripping my clothes off of me. Instead of scaring me, their hunger just turns me on even more.

"Angel, we are your mates," the tallest of the three tells me while gently stroking my cheek. "We are going to mark you, pleasure you, and make you ours."

"Yes, please," I whisper. "Do whatever you want to me."

No sooner have I said that than the man takes my mouth in a ravenous kiss. He continues making love to my mouth while running his hands all over my body. I rub my hands up and down his chest before reaching for the hardness between his legs. It takes both of my hands to wrap around his girth. I give his cock a squeeze before working my hands down the length. Pre-cum is already spilling out, arousing me more. He pushes me down on the bed before sucking one nipple, then the other. It feels so good, but I need more. Then he puts his mouth against my pussy and devours it. He sucks on my clit, sending me spiraling. His beard is soaked with my juices. The other two get on either side of me, kissing my mouth, face, and neck before sucking my nipples and bringing my hands up to stroke both of their cocks.

So many mouths, hands, and cocks. All I feel is pleasure and the desperate need to be filled by them. I squirm under their ministrations; loving the sensations, but wanting so much more. They keep switching places so that everyone has a taste of my mouth, nipples, and pussy. Each of the men makes me come on their fingers and mouth. My screams of pleasure fill the room.

"We need to make you ours now," the sexy leader says while stroking his enormous cock.

"Yes, please!" I beg.

He moves over me and drives inside me with one hard thrust. I gasp at the sensation. It doesn't hurt as much as I had assumed it would. Instead, after a pinch of discomfort, I feel so much pleasure, it overwhelms me. With each thrust of his hips, I orgasm, soaking the bed with my cum. The others watch, waiting their turns and stroking their cocks.

"We are going to breed you tonight, sweetness," he whispers as he slams his cock into me again and again. As he lets go, he bites my nipple and pinches my clit. I scream as I orgasm again and feel him release stream after stream of cum into my hungry pussy. I know that he is right. These three incredibly virile men are going to get me pregnant tonight, and the thought amps up my desire even more.

He gives me a deep, passionate kiss before moving away from me. The second man takes his place. "Turn around, sweetheart. Up on all fours."

He kisses me gently before stroking my ass and pussy, working me into a frenzy with his fingers. I do as instructed and am rewarded with his cock filling me completely from behind. He pulls me against him and slams into me so hard, it almost hurts, but I want more. "Please don't hold back," I tell him. Apparently, that's all he needs to hear. He lifts me up and slams into me, again and again. As with his brother, my orgasms bleed into each other until I don't know where one ends and another begins. He holds me against him as he releases his cum inside me.

I am worn out, but I know the last man is still waiting for me, and I want him just as desperately as I wanted the other two. He motions for me to stand. I gasp as he picks me up like a rag doll and starts fucking me standing up, impaling me on his hard cock again and again until I'm running out of breath. I come continuously as he slams me down onto his cock over and over again. He releases inside me and gently lowers me to the bed. I'm surrounded by the three of them. They each reveal their sharp teeth, and lower them to my body; biting me at the same time. The ecstasy rolls through me so strongly, I pass out.

So, you see what I mean? Seriously, how is a wimpy little teenage boy going to compare to my three sexy bear shifters? Every time I dream about them, I wake up extremely horny and dripping from orgasms. All I can think about is having their hard cocks inside of me.

I've told my parents about my dreams. Well, not the specifics, but they pretty much get the gist. They are very open minded, and, frankly, don't seem as disturbed by the whole idea as you would think. That's why they are supporting my coming here today. I had a different dream last night; well, more like a flash. It showed a sign that said Landry National Park, so that's where I am now. It's a few hours from my house in Lambert, Colorado, but I feel like I'm supposed to be here. So I'm here. Hiking. Not my thing at all, but it really is beautiful here. I've seen some wild animals-deer, squirrels, and even a fox, but no bears yet. Are my shifters here? I really hope so. You have no idea how badly I want to meet and (let's be real) fuck my very sexy mates. I feel like I am getting closer to finding them.

I take a moment to appreciate the beauty surrounding me. This forest really is breathtaking. I don't think I've been anywhere so lovely before. I'm surrounded by mountains. It somehow makes me feel a sense of peace I've never felt anyplace else.

I've only been walking for a couple of hours, but I'm suddenly exhausted. I see smoke through the trees. I walk into a clearing and see the most perfect log cabin imaginable. Its wrap around porch and rocking chairs look so inviting. "It's stunning," I breathe reverently. Maybe the people inside will take pity on me, and let me lie down and take a nap. I knock on the door several times, but no one answers. "Hello?" I say, trying the doorknob. It's unlocked. I walk in and find that the cabin is even more impressive on the inside. The soaring wood ceilings are probably twenty feet tall. The cabin is almost all one massive room with a chef's kitchen, spacious living room, and the biggest bed I've ever seen. There's something vaguely familiar about it, but I'm too tired to think about what it might be. I try it out. It is the softest, most comfortable mattress I have ever felt. It feels like I'm lying on a fluffy cloud. I smile and fall immediately into a deep slumber.

Available on Amazon

# About the Author

Lacy Jane is a happily married empty nester and dog mom who believes in happily ever afters, and has always wanted to write steamy romances. She enjoys reading, streaming shows, hanging out with her husband, kids, friends, family, and dogs, traveling, shopping, and drinking delicious coffee drinks. She is obsessed with beauty products, and spends way too much time and money in Sephora and Ulta. Her books are for those who like their happily ever after a little on the dirty side.

You can connect with me on:

🌐 http://lacy-jane.mailchimpsites.com

🔗 https://www.amazon.com/author/lacyjane

Subscribe to my newsletter:

✉ http://lacy-jane.mailchimpsites.com

My books are for those who like their happily ever after a little on the dirty side. Always a steamy read with HEA guaranteed. Enjoy!

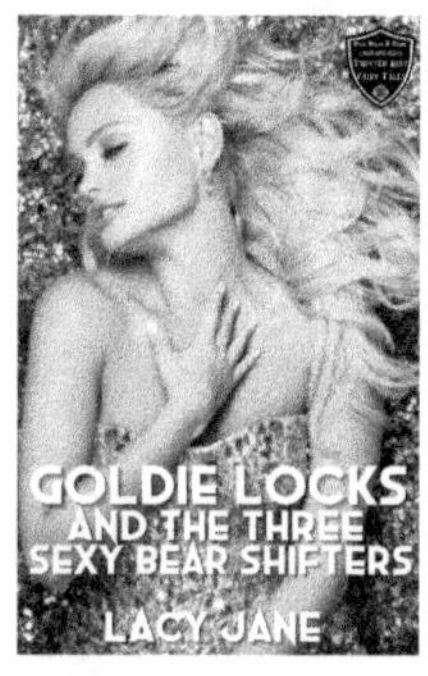

Goldie Locks and the Three Sexy Bear Shifters: A Steamy Reverse Harem Romance (Once Upon a Time-Twisted Sexy Fairy Tales Book 1)
Once upon a time, there was a girl named Goldie Locks who had very sexy dreams...

Every night, Goldie has dreams about her fated mates- three sexy bear shifters, but wakes every morning alone and longing for them. When she finally finds her beasts, they are ravenous for her. The sexy, possessive brothers will show her what it's like to be loved by three passionate shifters who are obsessed with their mate.

This very adult fairy tale is hot, hot, hot! Three sexy shifters, a strong heroine who knows what she wants, and (of course!) a HEA. My books are for those who like their happily ever after a little on the dirty side. A steamy read with HEA guaranteed. Enjoy!

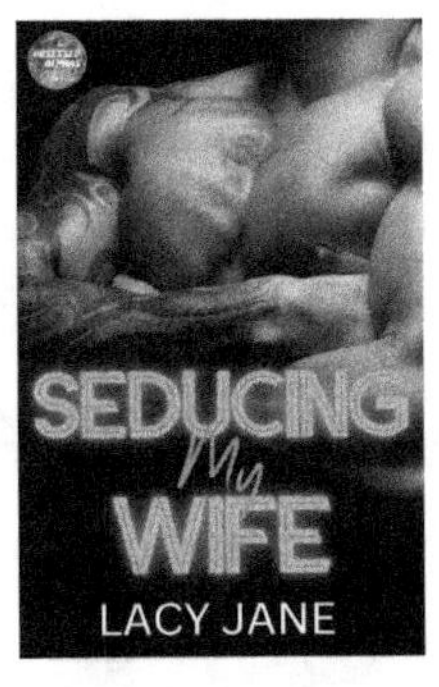

Seducing My Wife (Obsessed Alphas Book 2)
Can Jace convince Chloe to give him a second chance?
Find out if this very passionate couple can resolve their
differences in this quick, steamy read.

Jace

When I first saw my curvy wife, it was love and lust at first sight. She was everything I'd ever wanted. She was sweet, funny, gorgeous, and our chemistry was off the charts. We've been married for five years now. I have a successful business, and Chloe has a great career. I spend my days working and my nights inside my gorgeous wife. I thought everything was perfect. I assumed Chloe thought so, too, until she left me. Now I'm a shell of a man. The only thing that will make me whole again is Chloe. I will do everything I can to seduce my wife back into our bed and my life.

Chloe

I've loved Jace since the moment I saw him, but the last year or so, I've felt neglected. It's not another woman. It's his company. It takes up more and more of his time. It bothered me before, but now I have more than myself to think of. I left Jace to figure out what is best for both of us, but I have a secret. I hope he won't be too upset when he finds out what I've been hiding from him.

This book is high heat, no cheating, instalove, and (of course) a HEA. My books are for those who like their happily ever after a little on the dirty side. A steamy read with HEA guaranteed. Enjoy!

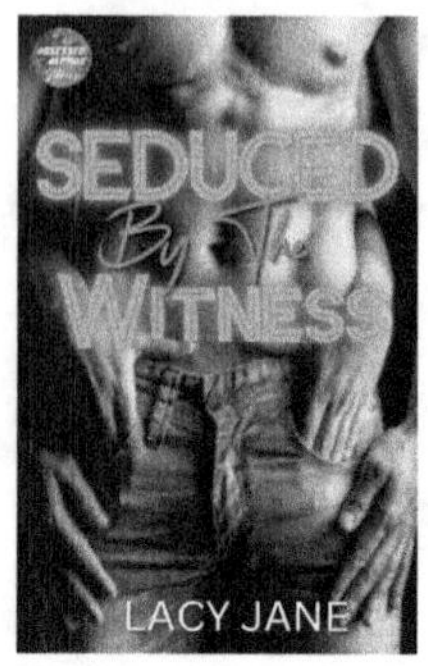

Seduced by the Witness (Obsessed Alphas Book 1)
When a sexy FBI agent and a curvy, gorgeous witness are thrown together, sparks fly. Can they resist each other, or will they give in to their desires? Find out in this steamy, close proximity romance.

Evan

Faith is the one. I knew it the second I laid eyes on her. In my job as an FBI agent, I've always remained professional-until now. Faith is the only witness to a murder, but she is temptation personified. I just need to keep my hands to myself until we catch the killer; then all bets are off. She belongs to me. She just doesn't know it yet.

Faith

After witnessing a murder, I meet the hottest man I've ever seen. Evan is tall, dark, handsome, and keeps me in a constant state of arousal. I'm scared to death, but he makes me feel safe. He says we have to wait because he's protecting me, but can he be seduced by the witness?

This book has instalove, high heat, no cheating, and (of course!) a HEA. My books are for those who like their happily ever after a little on the dirty side. A steamy read with HEA guaranteed. Enjoy!

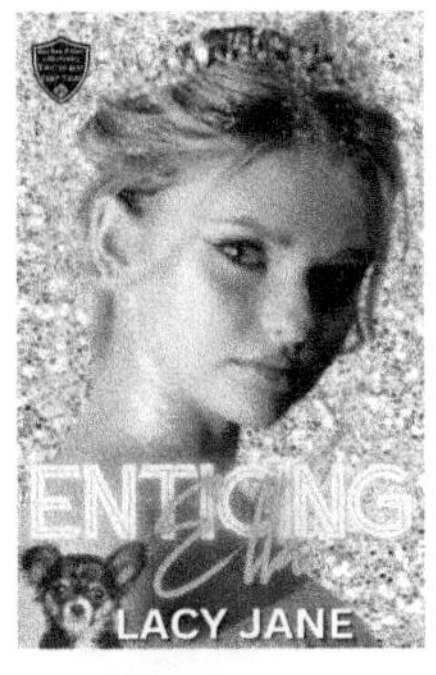

Enticing Ella (Once Upon a Time: Twisted Sexy Fairy Tales Book 3)

After a night of passion with Prince, Ella disappears. Now that Prince has claimed Ella, he will stop at nothing to find her and make her his bride. Can he save her from her evil stepmother in time? Find out in this sweet, spicy, modern version of Cinderella, complete with a ball, one evil stepmother, a fairy godmother of sorts, and Ella's adorable little dog, Cujo.

As with all of my books, this OTT romance contains high heat, instalove, no cheating, and (of course!) a HEA. Always a steamy read with HEA guaranteed. Enjoy!

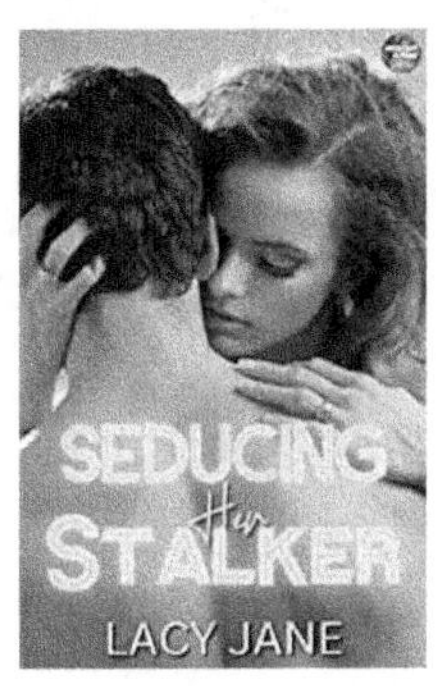

Seducing Her Stalker (Obsessed Alphas Book 3)

Can a stalker find happiness with the object of his obsession?

From the moment Jaxon sees Serena, he becomes completely obsessed with her. His life suddenly revolves around the sweet, sexy librarian. He finds himself crossing more and more lines as his obsession intensifies. When he finds out she returns his feelings, he is determined to make her his. Will she still feel the same if she finds out how deep his obsession with her is?

Like all of my books, this is an OTT instalove with high heat, no cheating, and (of course!) a HEA. If you are looking for a squeaky clean romance, I am not your girl. If you like your romance a little on the dirty side, read away! Always a steamy read with HEA guaranteed. Enjoy!